Tale Of A One Way Street

by
Joan Aiken

WITHDRAWN FROM STOCK

RED FOX

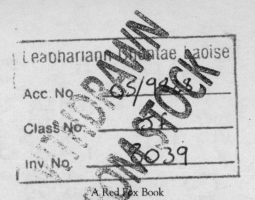

Leabharlann Bhuntae Laoise

Acc. No. 05/92 ___

Class No. ___

Inv. No. 6039

A Red Fox Book

Published by Random House Children's Books
20 Vauxhall Bridge Road, London, SW1V 2SA

A division of Random House UK Ltd
London Melbourne Sydney Auckland
Johannesburg and agencies throughout the world

Copyright © text Joan Aiken Enterprises Ltd, 1978
Copyright © illustrations Jan Pienkowski, 1978

1 3 5 7 9 10 8 6 4 2

First published in Great Britain by
Jonathan Cape Limited 1978

This Red Fox edition 1999

This book is sold subject to the condition that it shall not, by way of trade or
otherwise, circulated without the publisher's prior consent in any form of binding
or cover other than that in which it is published and without a similar condition
including this condition being imposed on the subsequent purchaser.

The right of Joan Aiken and Jan Pienkowski to be identified as
the author and illustrator of this work has been asserted by them
in accordance with the Copyright, Design and Patents Act, 1988.

Printed and bound in Great Britain by
Cox & Wyman Ltd, Reading, Berkshire

Papers used by Random House UK Limited are natural, recyclable products
made from wood grown in sustainable forests. The manufacturing processes
conform to the environmental regulations of the country of origin.

RANDOM HOUSE UK Limited Reg. No. 954009

ISBN 0 09 940233 5

CONTENTS

Tale of a One-Way-Street   7

The Lions   21

The Alarm Cock   33

The Tractor, the Duck and the Drum   48

The Queen of the Moon   67

Tale of a One-Way Street

THERE WAS A little town which had a one-way street in it. In this town also, the postman carried a walkie-talkie radio set, so that as he went along the streets, putting people's letters through their front doors, he could report all the news back to the post office.

'Mrs Jones got a postcard from her son in Rome. And she's having fried eggs for breakfast.'

'Mr Smith's parcel of fish-hooks has come at last. But one of his front windows is broken; it looked as if a bird had flown into it.'

'Miss Brown's mother in Ipswich sent her a currant cake. Very good; she just gave me a piece. And her white cat has had kittens in front of the kitchen fire: two, at present.'

The people in the post office, who had to spend all day sorting letters into little heaps, one heap for each street, were very pleased to get all this interesting news while they did their dull job.

One morning the postman said,

'I'm at the top of the one-way street. There's a mover's van halfway down the hill. I reckon a new family is moving into the empty house. I'll tell you more later.'

And he started down the one-way street, putting letters through people's letter-boxes as he went along.

The name of this street was really Narrow Hill. Because it was so narrow, and so steep, the traffic was only allowed to go down it, never up, and so everyone in the town had fallen into the habit of calling it the one-way street, instead of using its proper name.

'Good morning,' said the postman to the new family who were moving their furniture out of the van. 'Any letters for you, I wonder?'

'Mann, the name is,' said the father. 'Mr and Mrs Mann. And young Tom Mann.'

'Number Fifty, Mr and Mrs Mann,' said the postman writing it down. 'No letters today, but perhaps there'll be some tomorrow.'

Mr Mann stuck up a sign that said, T. MANN, PLUMBER. Mrs Mann carried in a last load of sheets and towels. Then the mover's van drove off.

When young Tom Mann put his head out of the front door, after helping to carry in all the furniture, a thrush flying past overhead called, 'Hullo, young Tom Mann! You must turn right!'

And a horse trotting past, pulling a cart full of beer barrels, called, 'Turn right, Tom Mann, turn right, clippety-clop, turn right.'

'Why must I turn right?' said Tom. 'If I turn right, that takes me down to the bottom of the hill. But I want to go up to the top.'

'You must turn right because it is a one-way street,' said the postman, walking on down the hill, putting letters into people's boxes.

'Good morning, I'm the postman with one-way feet,
And I walk one way along the one-way street.'
The thrush, flying overhead, called,
'I'm the bird that nests in your garden and sings,
And I fly along the one-way street on one-way wings.'
A boy riding past on his bike shouted,
'I'm Bill, with a bike with a brake that squeals,
I bike along the one-way street on one-way wheels.'
A girl skated down the road on roller-skates, calling as she went,
'I'm Susan, a girl who never stands and waits,
I skate along the one-way street on one-way skates.'
A coal-man with a lorry delivering coal

called down from his driver's cab,
    'I'm the coal-man who carries in the
    coal for your fires,
    I drive along the one-way street on
    one-way tyres.'
A cat, hurrying along the garden walls,
stopped to say,
    'I catch nice mice in my clever claws,
    And I trot along the one-way street on
    one-way paws.'
A gull called down from high up,
    'I float one way over all the roofs,'
and the horse, pulling his beer cart,
neighed,
    'I canter one way on my one-way hoofs.'
And the sun, high overhead in the sky,
winked its great golden eye as a cloud

sailed past underneath, and said,

'I'm the sun who shines in the sky so
bright,

I travel one way from morning to night.'

'But what happens if I want to go the
other way?' said Tom.

'You'd get run over and squashed flat,'
said the postman.

'All the birds would bump into you,' said
the thrush.

'So would the horses,' said the horse.

'You'd get lost and never come home
again,' said Bill and Susan.

'Nobody ever *has* gone the other way,'
said the coal-man. 'It's not allowed.'

'I don't see why,' said Tom, but at that
moment his mother put her head out of
the front door and said, 'Tom, it's time for
dinner, and don't let me hear any talk
about your going the wrong way along the
one-way street. Why, goodness knows
where you'd end up! At the North Pole,
most likely!'

So Tom went in to dinner, and all the
other people went their way down the hill,
skating or walking or driving or biking or
flying or trotting.

But Tom kept thinking about the one-way
street as he ate his boiled egg. Boiled eggs

and bread-and-butter was what they had
for lunch, because of having just moved
into the house. Mrs Mann had not had time
to get to the shops yet.

'Mother,' said Tom, 'how do you boil an
egg?'

'There's only one way to boil an egg
properly,' said his mother. 'You put it into
boiling water and wait till it's done.

    You could keep on boiling eggs all day,
    But still there's only one right way.'

'And how do you make bread and butter?'
said Tom.

'There's only one way. You put the butter
on the bread and spread it.

    Take loaf, take butter, and cut, and
    spread,
    There's only one way to put butter on
    bread.'

'How do you mend a burst pipe?' Tom
asked his father.

'There's nobbut one way to do it properly,'
said Tom's father, and he told Tom how it
was done.

    'Smooth and solder and work and wipe,
    There's only one way to mend a pipe.'

Tom listened to his father and his mother
and he said to himself, 'I can see there's
only one way to boil an egg and spread

butter and mend a pipe, but there are *two* ways to walk along a street, and I don't see why I'm not allowed to use them both.'

But he didn't say this out loud. His mother was busy moving tables and chairs around, to see which way looked best, and his father was hard at work, deciding which things ought to go into which rooms.

Tom went and looked out through the front window at the one-way street. Every moving thing that he could see was going *down* the hill – cars and carts, prams and bikes, ladies and dogs and pushchairs and bakers' vans.

'Just the same,' thought Tom, 'some day I am going *up* that hill, to find out where it goes.'

Next day Tom went down the hill to school at the bottom. And there he learned to read.

'There's only one way to learn reading,' said the teacher. 'You have to start with letters.

There's just one way and that is that
C-A-T spells nothing but cat.'

Next Tom learned sums.

'There's only one way, there aren't any more
Two plus two makes only four.'

On his way home from school Tom thought harder than ever about the one-way street. He had to go home a different way, which took longer, along Traders' Lane, and Market Hill, and Church Walk, and Parson's Steps, which brought him out at the top of Narrow Hill, and then he could run down the street to his home.

Each day at school the lessons were just the same, until they came to Friday. On Friday they had painting, and the painting teacher was somebody new, somebody Tom had not seen before.

When Tom asked, 'What is the proper way to paint a picture?' this teacher said,

'There isn't any right way. There are hundreds of ways, and each one is different. You just have to take your courage in your hands and begin.'

Tom didn't know how to take his courage in his hands, but he took paper and brushes and paints, and he painted a picture of Narrow Hill, the one-way street, with the houses going right up the hill and off the top of the paper.

Susan looked over his shoulder and said, 'You silly boy! There ought to be *sky* at the top, not houses. And who ever heard of a *pink cat?*'

Bill looked over his shoulder and said, 'All the things in your picture are going the wrong way, if that is meant to be our street. And I never yet saw a dark-blue horse. You must be crazy!'

But the teacher looked at Tom's picture and said,

'You keep on exploring that avenue, boy, and you may find out a secret or two, by and by.'

Tom was surprised, because he thought his picture was of a street, not an avenue, but he was pleased when the teacher put it up on the wall and stuck a gold star on it.

Next morning was Saturday, so there was no school. It was a quiet, foggy, misty, grey, empty day which seemed to have no beginning or middle or end. The sun didn't even try to shine through the fog. Tom's mother was painting the bathroom walls, and his father was fixing the kitchen taps, both very busy, so Tom thought, 'Now is my chance.'

He put on his long woolly scarf, and he took his courage in both hands, now that he knew how, and he went out of the front door and turned left up the hill, into the thick, white, woolly fog. It was very queer, rather like being inside a white parcel, and at first Tom didn't much care for it.

But then he heard a pit-a-pat noise, and he saw a bright pink cat trotting along just ahead of him.

'Hullo, young Tom Mann,' said the cat. 'Going my way?'

'Yes, I think so, thank you,' said Tom, and he followed the pink cat.

Now beyond the pink cat he noticed a yellow seagull and a silver thrush, flying through the mist.

'Hullo, Tom,' they called. 'Are you going our way?'

'Yes, I believe so, thank you,' said Tom.

Next he saw a pea-green postman with a sack of mail, and a bright red coal-man, whose lorry was stacked with scarlet bags of coal.

'Good morning, Tom,' they said. 'Going our way, are you?'

'Yes, thank you,' said Tom. And then he saw a dark-blue horse, and a golden girl on rollerskates, and an orange boy on a bike.

'Hi there, Tom,' they called. 'Are you going our way?'

'Yes I am,' said Tom.

Then he came to the top of the hill. There was the sun, standing still overhead and shining bright violet rays down across the country on the other side of the hill. The fog stopped here like a wall. Tom, and all the people with him, could see for miles and miles into the land that lay beyond, but they could not see right across, because the country was far too wide.

What they could see was very surprising.

They saw a whole mountain of boiled eggs, each one different from all the others. They saw a whole field paved with slices of bread-and-butter, no two of them alike. They saw a great forest of pipes, each pipe mended in a different way. They saw streams and fountains of letters and numbers sparkling in the purple rays of the sun, making hundreds and thousands of different words, giving the answers to any number of sums. And all the words were right, and all were different. All the sums were right and all were different.

In the middle, on a sunny hillside, under a tree covered in cherries the size of apples, or apples the colour of cherries, was a comfortable chair with a label on it that said TOM.

'Now I know,' said Tom, to the cat and the gull and the thrush and the postman and the coal-man and the horse and the boy and the girl, 'that while I thought I was coming your way, *you* were all coming *my* way. And now I know about this place, I shall come here as often as I like.'

He sat down comfortably in the chair and watched three lemon-yellow fish jumping in the fountain, catching the numbers in their mouths.

The cat chased a pink mouse, the postman delivered half a dozen pea-green letters, and the dark-blue horse nibbled a clump of red primroses.

When Tom went home, he found his mother still painting the bathroom and his father still fixing the kitchen taps. Neither of them had noticed that he had been gone.

'Oh, Tom,' said his mother. 'Run down the hill, will you, and buy me a bottle of Jollyclens, that's the only stuff to get paint off paintbrushes.'

'And while you're at it,' said his father, 'get me a packet of Smith's Superfine Staples. Don't get any other kind.'

'Okay,' said Tom, and he took the money his mother gave him and went out of the front door, turning right and running down the steep hill, going the same way as all the cars and horses

and prams and bikes and vans and ladies
with their dogs. For now the fog had lifted
and he could see everything as plain as
plain.

He bought the Jollyclens and the Smith's
Superfine Staples, and went back, taking
the way he came after school, by Traders'
Lane, and Market Hill, and Church Walk,
and Parson's Steps, and so to the top of
Narrow Hill, from where he could run all
the way to his front door. And as he ran he
sang,

    'I'm Tom, the boy with one-way feet
    And I run one way along the one-way
    street.'

When he got home he gave his mother
the bottle of Jollyclens and he said to her,

'Mum.'

'Well?'

'You can't walk more than one way at a
time, can you?'

'Of course you can't,' said his mother.
'Don't be silly. And go and put on the kettle
for tea. I've made a very nice new kind of
cake. It's on the shelf in the larder.'

The postman, on his walkie-talkie set,
reported back to the post office,

'The new family, halfway up Narrow Hill,
seems to be settling in nicely.'

The Lions

IN THE MIDDLE of a town by a river there was once a little park, not much bigger than somebody's front garden. It was all paved with brick, and in the centre of it grew a weeping willow tree. Around the edge of the garden stood a row of red geraniums in pots. Along one side, beyond a white railing, flowed the green river, breaking into foamy ripples and waves in its hurry, sometimes throwing up sudden bursts of bubbles. And at each corner of the little park, facing inwards so that they could see one another comfortably, crouched four stone lions. One had moss growing on his tail. One had a swallow's nest of straw built between his ears. One had a broken paw, where a boy had thrown a brick. And somebody had written I LOVE FRANK on the fourth lion. But the word FRANK, down by his tail, had been nearly washed off by rain, and the word I was tangled up in his mane, so that if you glanced quickly, the lion seemed to have been labelled LOVE.

The four lions talked to each other all day long, without making a sound.

Over on the other side of the green rushing river was a huge rubbish dump; all the empty tins, broken bottles, old bones, torn newspapers and boxes, rotten vegetables, worn-out clothes, radio sets and shoes, damaged chairs, smashed plates, dead flowers, fish-heads, and unpaid bills that people in the town wanted to throw away, they rowed in boats across the river, or carried over the bridge, and flung on to this heap, which was now higher than any church in the town. When the sun was low the shadow of the heap stretched right over the water.

The lions had a friend who visited them in their garden every day. In fact they had two friends. Each afternoon an old man in a wheel-chair was brought there by his daughter, who left him for a couple of hours while she did her shopping. If the weather was fine, she left his chair close by the railing where he could most easily hear the river, for he was rather deaf. But if it rained, or was likely to, she left him under the weeping willow, which was even better than an umbrella.

The old man carried his canary with him, in a cage on his knee. Every day, the minute his daughter was out of sight, he opened the cage door and let the canary fly out. First it shot up into the willow tree

with a burst of song; then it
would fly to the railing and
look at the river; then it would
visit the lions, each in turn,
and take them the old man's
greetings. For the canary could
listen to the old man's thoughts,
and translate them into song;
and it could also hear what the lions
were thinking and carry their silent speech
to the old man. So every day these friends
would have a long, interesting conversation.

Sometimes the old man told the lions
about his life. He had been a sailor when he
was younger, travelling all over the world.
And the lions had had many adventures
too, for long ago, before they had been
brought to their present place, they had
kept guard over the tomb of a
great king in a desert land,
many thousands of miles
away, and for hundreds
of years they had
watched over the
comings and goings of
priests and noblemen
and common people
coming to pay their
respects at the tomb.

So there was always plenty to talk about, and the canary flew to and fro, making a pattern like a yellow star as it flashed from one corner of the garden to another, and back to the tree in the middle, taking a question or a joke or a thought from one friend to another as if it carried a bundle of words on its yellow back.

One day the old man was rather late.

'What can be keeping him?' said the moss-tailed lion.

'The sun is behind the church spire already,' said the straw-capped lion.

'The old man has been rather pale these last few days,' said the lion with the broken paw.

'Perhaps he is ill,' said the lion labelled LOVE.

'How long has he been coming to our garden?' said Moss Tail.'

'Only since they built the new bridge,' said Straw Cap. 'Thirty winters, no more.'

'A long time in men's counting,' said Broken Paw.

'Here he comes now,' said Love.

The old man's daughter wheeled him in and left him under the weeping willow, for the sky was grey. Today the old man was wrapped in a thick rug.

'Are you sure you will be all right, Father?' said the daughter. 'Will you be warm enough?'

'Yes, thank you, my dear.'

'I'll be back soon. I'll be as quick as I can.'

'Don't worry. Enjoy your shopping. I like to sit here,' he said, as she hurried away. And he opened the cage door and let out the canary, who darted like a yellow flash of sunshine to each lion in turn.

'The old man is not very well today,' he told them. 'I'm afraid that in the winter he won't be able to come to the garden any more.'

The lions were dismayed.

'How shall we be able to have our conversations? We shall miss him,' said Moss Tail.

'Can you fly to us from his house?' said Straw Cap.

'No, for his daughter won't let me out. She is afraid that I might be stolen, or get lost,' said the bird.

'Perhaps the old man can persuade her,' said Broken Paw.

'But if he is ill, the canary should stay with him,' said Love.

'Let us not waste time worrying about the

25

winter,' said the old man. 'Let us talk while we can, and finish as much as possible of what we have to say.'

'What shall we talk about today?' said Moss Tail.

'The rubbish dump,' said Straw Cap.

'Yes, we should certainly talk about that,' said Broken Paw. 'Today its shadow almost reaches across the river.'

'What can be done about it?' said Moss Tail.

'I have a suggestion,' said Love. 'Let me think about it a little longer so as to get it quite clear in my head.'

'Do you suppose people have made rubbish heaps like that all over the world?' said Straw Cap to the old man.

'Most probably,' he said.

'Then we should talk about them all,' said Broken Paw. 'What is your idea, Love?'

During this time the canary had been busily flying back and forth between the lions and the old man, rather like a spider spinning a web. Now, as the lion called Love was still not quite ready to explain his idea, the canary took a rest for a moment, perching on the railing by the river.

At this moment a man came rowing down the river. He had unloaded a whole boatful of broken television sets on to the rubbish dump and jumped back into his empty boat. Then, spying the canary, as a current carried him to that side of the river, he pulled a big red handkerchief out of his pocket, flung it over the bird, stuffed handkerchief, bird and all into a wicker basket he had in the boat, and was away down the river before either the old man or the lions realised what was happening.

Indeed the old man, who was very short-sighted, did not know that his canary had been stolen; he sat patiently waiting, expecting that in a moment or two the little bird would fly back to him with some thought from one of the lions.

The lions were terribly upset.

'Our translator has been kidnapped,' said Moss Tail.

'What shall we do?' said Straw Cap.

'We'll never be able to get him back,' said Broken Paw.

But we must try to,' said Love.

'Without him we can't talk to the old man,' said Moss Tail.

'And he can't talk to us,' said Straw Cap.

'We shall never be able to put our heads together and make a plan to get rid of the rubbish heap,' said Broken Paw.

'We need help,' said Love.

'What is happening?' said the old man. 'Why does nobody speak?'

'You can't hear us,' said Moss Tail.

'Oh, this is dreadfully sad,' said Straw Cap, and a stone tear as big as a tennis ball rolled down his nose and on to his paws.

'I don't see how we can be helped,' said Broken Paw.

But Love called up to a golden eagle flying overhead. 'Can you see a man in a boat with a basket? Is he still on the river?'

'Yes, I can see him,' said the golden eagle, hovering far up in the sunshine on his powerful wings. 'Why do you want to know? He is going down the river, heading for the sea.'

'He has made off with a friend of ours, a canary,' said Moss Tail.

'How can we prevent him getting away?' said Straw Cap.

'You could sink his boat,' said the golden eagle. 'I could easily overtake the boat and drop a heavy weight on it, if you can give me something suitable.'

'But what do we have?' said Moss Tail.

'My tear?' said Straw Cap.

'Not heavy enough,' said the golden eagle, after he had picked up the tear to test it.

'We have nothing else,' said Broken Paw. 'We have lost our only chance.'

'We have ourselves,' said Love.

'One of *us*?' said Moss Tail.

'But,' said Broken Paw, 'which ever one of us the golden eagle dropped would end up at the bottom of the river.'

'We are made of stone. Whoever it was would come to no harm,' said Love.

'It would be lonely down there,' said Moss Tail.

'How would he get back?' said Straw Cap.

'He might be down there for a hundred years,' said Broken Paw.

'We have no choice,' said Love.

'Why does nobody speak to me?' said the old man.

'We must hurry and do *something*,' said Moss Tail.

'Oh, this is terrible,' said Broken Paw, and he too dropped a stone tear.

'You'll have to be quick making up your minds,' said the golden eagle. 'The boat is getting very close to the sea.'

'Which of us shall it be?' said Love.

'I can't go because of the swallows nesting between my ears,' said Straw Cap.

'I might not be heavy enough, with my broken paw,' said Broken Paw.

'I haven't the courage,' said Moss Tail.

'Then I had better go,' said Love.

So the golden eagle flew to Love, and took a firm grip with his powerful claws on the lion's mane and tail.

He flapped his great wings and rose into the air, more slowly than usual, for Love was a massive weight, carved from pure marble.

'Goodbye,' called Moss Tail sadly.

'Goodbye,' called Broken Paw.

'Goodbye,'
called Straw Cap.

'Perhaps we shall see each other again,' said Love. Then the golden eagle dropped Love, who fell like a thunderbolt, smashing clean through the boat and sinking it instantly. And the thief was carried down with it and drowned.

But the golden eagle dived, almost as fast as Love fell, and snatched up the wicker basket which remained floating on the water. He flew back and laid the basket on the lap of the old man, who was very much surprised. He felt for the catch and let out the canary.

'Why, what has been happening to you, my poor bird?'

'Oh, sir!' said the canary. 'I have had such a narrow escape! A man in a boat grabbed me in a red cloth, and if, by some strange piece of luck, the boat had not sunk, and if, by some mysterious stroke of fortune, an eagle had not kindly picked me up, I should never have got back to you.'

'Well, and it is also very lucky that my daughter has not returned yet,' said the old man. 'For she is always saying that if I let you fly loose, somebody might steal you.

'But now let us make haste and hear what Love has to say about the rubbish dump: he will certainly have had time to collect his thoughts by now.'

However, just at that moment, the old man's daughter did come back, so the canary hurriedly hopped into his cage, the old man snapped the catch, and the daughter wheeled the pair of them away so fast that they did not realise one lion was gone; the canary was too flustered and the old man was too short-sighted.

'Will they come back tomorrow, do you think?' said Straw Cap.

'I wonder if we shall ever see Love again,' said Broken Paw.

After that there was silence in the garden for a long time, while each of the three thought his own thoughts, and the river rushed by.

And below the rushing green water, deep down on the sandy bottom at the river's mouth, Love lay motionless, with his head on his paws, patiently waiting until somebody should come to rescue him.

The Alarm Cock

ONCE THERE WAS a shop with a sign over the door that said, VINE, WOLF, AND PARROTT, HELPERS.

If you opened the door and went in, you saw the Vine right away, for it grew out of the floor and up the walls of the little shop, so the whole room was lined with leaves, and clusters of flowers hung from the ceiling. Beautiful orange trumpet-shaped flowers they were, and the vine was covered with them all the year round.

The next thing you saw was Wolf. He was a real wolf, big and grey, with a handsome ruff round his neck, and he sat on the counter looking thoughtful and wise, with his long chin sunk on his shaggy grey chest.

And the last thing you saw was old Mr Parrott, who was not a bird but a grey-haired old man, generally at work in some corner of the shop, pruning the vine, or twining a new shoot so that it would grow comfortably up the wall.

Another sign, over the counter, said, NO FEES UNLESS SATISFIED.
PAYMENT IN KIND ACCEPTED.
WE HELP YOU WITH YOUR PROBLEMS.

33

And it was true, there were not many
problems that the firm of Vine, Wolf, and
Parrott could not solve.

For instance one day a man came in to
complain, 'My dog sits up on the roof all
day. Even at night he won't come down.
What's the use of a dog who's never in the
house and won't even come for a walk? Is
something wrong with him?'

'Does he bark or howl?' asked Wolf.

'No, just sits watching the clouds and the
birds.'

'Wolf had better go and talk to him,' said
old Mr Parrott. 'What is your address?'

'Eighty-four Smith Street.'

So old Mr Parrott got out his bicycle, and
a ladder, and bicycled along to Number
Eighty-four Smith Street, with the ladder on
his shoulder and Wolf sitting on one end of
it, and he held the foot of the ladder while
Wolf climbed up on to the roof to talk to the
dog, and soon found out that he was
annoyed because his master never watched
greyhound racing on television, and so he
had gone on a roof-strike, but would agree
to come down if he might sometimes be
allowed to watch his favourite TV
programme.

A man came in to say, 'My car has caught

a cold. It keeps sneezing. What should I do?'

'Get it a warmer bonnet. And put socks on its tyres. And give it a basinful of this Car Cough Mixture night and morning.'

A girl came in to say, 'My record player has slowed down. Instead of the record going round thirty-three times and a half every minute, it goes round once every thirty-three and a half minutes. What can I do about it?'

'You can slow down too,' said old Mr Parrott, after consulting his partners. 'Swallow this slow-down pill and then you'll be able to hear the music just as well as before.'

The girl swallowed the pill, and it slowed her down so much that it took her half an hour to walk to the door of the shop, and she hasn't reached home yet.

An old lady who lived just along the street, Mrs Heyhoe, came in with her little grand-daughter. Mrs Heyhoe was called Anna, so was her grand-daughter, and there were exactly seventy years between them. One was seven, the other seventy-seven. And they both looked the same; fair hair, bright blue eyes, straight noses, rather short, very cheerful.

'What can I do for you, Mrs Heyhoe, ma'am?' said old Mr Parrott, while little Anna patted Wolf, who wagged his tail.

'I can't get to sleep, Mr Parrott. I haven't slept a wink these three weeks.'

'Dear me,' said Mr Parrott. 'That's serious, that is. What you need is a nutmeg-scented fan. Buy a fan, soak it in nutmeg essence, fan yourself a hundred times, and that should do the trick.'

'Shall I pay you now?' said old Mrs Heyhoe.

'No, no,' he said, pointing to the sign, 'not until you are satisfied.'

So old Mrs Heyhoe went down the road to a fan shop, where she and little Anna chose a very pretty fan, lace, painted all over with roses.

They ground up a hundred nutmegs in the mincer and made a strong nutmeg tea. They sprinkled the fan with nutmeg tea three times an hour for three days, and then at bedtime old Mrs Heyhoe fanned herself a hundred times. Then little Anna fanned her a hundred times. Then she fanned herself again. Little Anna went to sleep, but her grandmother stayed wide awake all night until the sun came in the kitchen window and turned all the teacloths pink.

She thought of all sorts of useful things during the night: where she had put her glasses, a way to use up all her old stockings by stuffing cushions with them, and five new ideas for puddings, but she went back to Mr Parrott, and said,

'The nutmeg fan didn't work.'

'Dear me,' he said. 'It's not often that one of our suggestions doesn't work. Then you had better try playing the flute for half an hour, last thing before you go to bed, with your feet in a big bowl of honey.'

Mrs Heyhoe tried that. She already had a flute that her son, Anna's father, had played when he was a boy. And she kept bees, so she had plenty of honey.

But her next-door neighbour came to the back door, knocking, just when Mrs Heyhoe had got her feet into the honey, to say that Anna's father had called up on her telephone, and was wishful to speak to his mum, who hadn't got a phone.

So that was a nuisance, and it took Mrs Heyhoe quite a long time to get the honey from between her toes, and even so some got spilt on the kitchen floor, and after all, her son only wanted to know if little Anna was behaving herself.

'Which I am, aren't I, Granny?' said little Anna.

'Beautifully, my dearie.'

Then they found that the flute had fallen into the honey.

And that night again Mrs Heyhoe didn't sleep a wink.

'Really,' said old Mr Parrott, when she went back to him next day. 'I don't know that we've ever had a more awkward case. You had better try sniffing at a clove orange, while at the same time imagining that you are inside a teapot.'

So Mrs Heyhoe and Anna bought a whole lot of cloves and made two clove oranges (one for little Anna to take to her mother when she went home). They stuck the cloves all over the oranges, so tight together that you couldn't get a pin between them.

Mrs Heyhoe's kitchen smelt delicious, with the oranges, and the cloves, and the honey, and the nutmeg fan, which they had put up over the fireplace.

At bedtime Mrs Heyhoe shut her eyes and sniffed one of the oranges, and imagined that she was inside a teapot.

But next morning she went back to Vine, Wolf and Parrott.

'It didn't work,' she told Mr Parrott. 'That was the dirtiest teapot I've ever been inside. I had to spend the whole night scrubbing to get it clean. Never had a wink of sleep the whole night long.'

'Humph,' said old Mr Parrott. 'This certainly is a serious case.'

He consulted again with his partners.

'If we could find out *why* Mrs Heyhoe can't get to sleep,' said the Vine in her soft voice, 'we might be able to suggest the cure for her trouble.'

When the Vine spoke, her voice came out through all of her trumpet-shaped orange flowers.

'*Why* can't you get to sleep, ma'am?' asked old Mr Parrott.

'Because I'm so worried about waking up in time,' said old Mrs Heyhoe.

'Then,' said the Vine, 'what she needs is an alarm cock.'

'What's that?' said little Anna.

'A rooster alarm clock. You've heard of a cuckoo clock? A rooster clock is just the same. Only, instead of going Cuckoo, it goes Cock-a-doodle-doo, and wakes you up.'

'Well,' said old Mrs Heyhoe, 'we had better get one.'

So she and little Anna walked all over the town, going to each clock shop in turn. But nowhere could they find a rooster alarm clock. They could find owl clocks and pigeon clocks, nightingale clocks and ostrich clocks, peacock clocks, lark, duck, and chick clocks, moorcock, blackcock and woodcock clocks, but not a single shop had a plain cock clock.

'I wonder,' said little Anna presently, 'if just an ordinary rooster wouldn't do as well, like the one Daddy has at home?'

40

TEMPUS FUGIT

'But where should we find a rooster in the town?' said her granny.

'Well,' said little Anna, 'as we walk along, I'm sure I can sometimes hear a rooster going Cock-a-doodle-doo.'

'It would be a funny thing if you could,' said her granny, 'right in the middle of the town.' But she began to listen, she listened and she listened, and by and by she thought she could hear a rooster somewhere going Cock-a-doodle-doo.

'It seems to be loudest in this street,' said little Anna.

They were in Smith Street.

They walked north, and the crowing got fainter. So then they walked west, along Jones Street, and it grew louder. Then it grew fainter, so they walked south along Brown Street, till it grew louder. Then it grew fainter, so they walked east along Robinson Street.

'Now we're back where we began, in Smith Street,' said little Anna.

'It's a puzzle,' said old Mrs Heyhoe.

'*I* believe the rooster's up above,' said little Anna.

They looked up. They had been walking round a big building which took up a whole city block. The building was fifty storeys high – so high that, as it was a misty day, the top was out of sight in the clouds.

'*I* think we'll have to go up,' said little Anna.

So they walked through the main entrance of the building, and went up. They went up in a lift, and at each floor they stepped out and asked the people there,

'Do you know of a rooster living on this floor?'

Nobody knew of a rooster – not on the fifth floor, nor the tenth, nor the twentieth, nor the twenty-fifth, nor the thirtieth, nor the fortieth.

At last they reached the fiftieth

floor and stepped out through a little door on to the roof, right above the clouds.

And there on the roof was a tiny cottage, with an old man sitting in the doorway peeling potatoes, and beside the door in the sunshine, sitting on an upside-down basket, was a beautiful glossy red rooster, with black and green feathers in his wings, and a black, blue, and green tail, and black legs, and a red cockscomb.

Little Anna ran to the cottage door.

'Oh, please,' she said to the old man, busy peeling his potatoes, 'could we buy your rooster?'

'Cock-a-doodle-doo!' shouted the rooster indignantly. 'Nobody's going to buy me!'

'No indeed!' said the old man. 'How would I be able to wake in the mornings without my rooster?'

'Besides,' said the rooster, 'I'm happy up here above the clouds. I wouldn't *dream* of living down below where it's all misty and grey. Up here the sun shines all day and the moon shines all night.'

Little Anna and her granny looked at each other sadly.

'They are right, you know,' said old Mrs Heyhoe. 'Why should the old man lose his rooster? And why should the rooster live below the clouds if he doesn't want to?'

But little Anna thought again and said to the old man, 'I suppose we couldn't *rent* your rooster, just for a week or two, till my granny gets into the habit of sleeping again?'

And she said to the rooster, 'The sun does shine down there sometimes. And Granny makes very good mashed potato.'

'Why, if you put it like that,' said the old man, whose name was Mr Welladay, 'that doesn't sound such a bad idea. In fact it sounds like a very *good* idea. I've been feeling rather tired lately; I could do with a few weeks' sleep.'

'Well,' said the rooster, whose name was Enrico, 'since you put it that way, that doesn't sound like a bad idea at all. In fact it would be very pleasant to get down out of the hot sun for a week or two.'

'What sort of rent would you like?' asked old Mrs Heyhoe.

'How about a nice chocolate cake?' asked old Mr Welladay.

So they went home, back down the lift, back along the street, with Enrico sitting on little Anna's shoulder. And Mrs Heyhoe at once baked a nice big chocolate cake, and little Anna took it back to Mr Welladay, who just had time to eat it before he fell fast asleep.

That evening, after they had all had supper – Enrico had cornflakes and milk, so did little Anna – old Mrs Heyhoe, too, fell fast asleep in her armchair, and slept there the whole night through, very peacefully, until Enrico woke her at seven next morning, shouting, 'Cock-a-doodle-doo! It's time to wake up and make my breakfast.'

Every night for seven nights old Mrs Heyhoe slept soundly. And every morning for seven mornings, Enrico woke her in the same way. On the eighth morning, he woke her by shouting,

'Cock-a-doodle-doo! It's time to get up and put little Anna on the train to go home!'

'Oh, thank goodness you woke me,' said old Mrs Heyhoe. 'I've been worrying about getting Anna on to that train this month past.'

'Is *that* why you couldn't sleep while I've been staying with you, Granny?' said little Anna.

'Of course it is!' said old Mrs Heyhoe.

So they walked to the station, and little Anna got on to the train, with her bag of clothes, and a sandwich, and an apple, and the clove orange for her mother, and she blew a kiss and waved and called out, 'Goodbye, Granny! Thank you for the lovely visit!'

Then old Mrs Heyhoe went along to Vine, Wolf, and Parrott, to thank them for their help. She had made another chocolate cake to pay them, as Mr Welladay had enjoyed his so much. Mr Parrott shared it with Wolf, as the Vine did not eat cake.

And then Mrs Heyhoe took Enrico back to old Mr Welladay, who had enjoyed his long sleep so much that he said, 'You are welcome to borrow my rooster again whenever your grand-daughter comes to visit. If Enrico agrees, of course.'

'Certainly I agree,' said Enrico. 'Mrs Heyhoe makes the best mashed potato I ever tasted. And little Anna polished my comb every night. Whenever her grand-daughter is here on a visit, I'll be glad to oblige Mrs Heyhoe.'

'And I'll be glad to have you,' said Mrs Heyhoe.

So that is what they did.

The Tractor, the Duck and the Drum

ONCE THERE WAS a boy called Euan, and it was going to be his birthday next week. He wanted a tractor that he could sit on, and it would go chug-chugging along. He wanted a drum that he could play on, rub-a-dub, rub-a-dub. And he wanted a real live duck that would swim in his bath and go quack, quack.

So he sat down and wrote a letter to his Aunt Bertha. His Aunt Bertha kept a wishing-spoon in her kitchen drawer. Wishing-spoons have a little shape like a shield at the back, where the spoon part joins on to the handle, so they look like this:

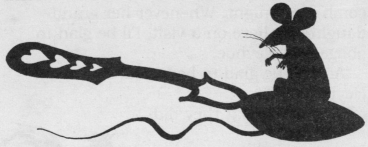

If you stir a cake, before it is cooked, with a wishing-spoon, there is a good chance that your wish will come true.

So Euan wrote to his Aunt Bertha:

DERE ANT BIRTHDAY
I SHD BEE VERRY GREAT
FULL IF U CD SEND MEE
A TRACK TOR

I CAN RIDE ON WAT GOES
CHUG CHUG CHUG & A
DRUM

I CAN PLAY ON
WAT GOES RUB A DUB DUB
& A DUK

TO SWIM IN MY BARF
WAT GOES QUAK QUAK QUAK
HOPE YOR ROOM A TIZ BETR
LUV FRUM EUAN

and he folded the letter neatly in four, and put it in an envelope, and put a stamp on it, and posted it off to his Aunt Bertha.

His Aunt Bertha was a very absent-minded lady, and she was hasty, too. When the letter came she put down her knitting and she took her scissors and she slit the envelope open, and by doing that she cut Euan's letter into four bits.

'Here's a letter from my birthday nephew,'

said Aunt Bertha. 'Let's see what he wants.'

She took the four bits of paper and put them in a row, and read them.

'Now here's a puzzle,' said Aunt Bertha. 'For he seems to want a duck he can ride on that will go rub-a-dub-dub. And he wants a tractor he can play on that will go quack-quack-quack. And he seems to want a drum that will swim in his bath and go chug-chug-chug. Who ever heard of a drum going chug-chug-chug? And I am sure it would not be at all good for a drum to put it in the bath.'

Then she moved the four bits of paper into a different row, and read them again.

'But perhaps he wants a drum he can ride on that will go quack-quack-quack? Or a duck he can play on that will go chug-chug-chug? Or a tractor to swim in his bath and go rub-a-dub-dub?

'But I never heard of playing on a duck; it would have to be a very good-natured duck to stand being played on, surely?

'And how would you ride on a drum?

'As for putting a tractor in the bath, it would certainly have to be a HUGE bath, and even so the sides might get scratched.

'But as Euan is my only nephew, and as he has written to me so politely, I shall have to see what I can do.'

So Aunt Bertha put away her knitting,
and she took flour and baking powder and
nutmeg and cinnamon, she took butter and
sugar and eggs and milk and raisins and
currants and sultanas and nuts and dates
and figs and cherries and candied orange
and lemon peel, and she mixed all these
things together in a beautiful big bowl with
a brown outside and a white inside. She
mixed them and she stirred them, round
and round, to and fro, up and down, back
and forth, a hundred and three times over,
with her wishing-spoon.

She put a little old magic silver sixpence
into the mixture, and she stirred that in
too, a hundred and three times.

Then she poured all the brown, gloopy,
spicy mixture into a cake-tin, and baked
it in the oven for a hundred and three
minutes, until it smelt fruity and spicy and
sweet, like Christmas and Easter and
birthdays all mixed together.

Aunt Bertha took the cake out of the oven
and turned the tin upside down so that the
cake slid out on to a plate. Then she let it
get cool. Then she turned it the right way
up and iced it all over with white sugar
mixed with egg-white, and she decorated

the cake with a little tractor, and a little
drum, and a little duck, all made out of
white sugar. And in pink on top of the cake,
she wrote the words,

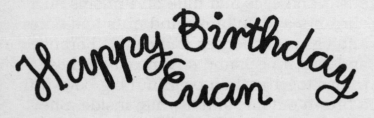

and then she wrapped the cake in paper
and put it in a box and stuck on a label
that said,
THIS WAY UP. PLEASE DO NOT BANG
OR BUMP. KEEP AWAY FROM MICE.
and she wrote Euan's name and address on
the side and posted it off at the post office.
The cake reached Euan quite safely and
he had it for his birthday-evening tea.
Everybody had a slice, and it was the
best cake they had eaten in their whole
lives.
And, in Euan's slice, he found the little
old magic silver sixpence. There was also a
note from Aunt Bertha, a bit brown from
having been baked.

Dear Euan, you should put the sixpence

under your pillow when you go to bed. It might be a good thing to put the tractor and the duck and the drum under your pillow too. My rheumatism is much better, thank you. Your loving Aunt Bertha.

PS. Then tomorrow, on your birthday, see what you get!

So when Euan went to bed he put the sixpence, the sugar tractor, the sugar duck, and the sugar drum, all under his pillow.

It took him a long time to go to sleep because he was excited.

In the middle of the night he woke up.

The moon was shining like daylight, and his pillow looked like a great snowy hill. Round the hill, chugging slowly along through the snow, came a huge white duck. And down the hill, rolling over and over, going rub-a-dub-dub, came a middle-sized tractor. And over the hill in the moonlight, flying against the blue starry sky, Euan saw a white drum that went quack, quack.

'There's been a muddle somewhere,' he thought.

The great white duck chugged up to Euan and smiled at him with its big smiling yellow beak and gave him a loving look out of its bright, black twinkling eye.

'I'm your friendly duck
Come to bring you
luck,' it said, 'with the
compliments of your Aunt
Bertha.'
The tractor rolled to a
stop in the snow beside
Euan and began to play a
tune like a musical box.
'Ting-a-ling, ding-a-ling,
listen to me sing
I'm your faithful
tractor, sound in limb
and wing.'
The drum floated down
beside them and perched
on a heap of snow.
'Quack quack, I'm your
loving drum, quack,
quack, quack
Any time you want a
ride, climb upon my
back.'
'There's certainly been
a muddle,' said Euan. 'But
never mind, let's go.'
And he climbed on to the
drum and began rolling it
along with his feet. This is
not at all an easy thing to

do, but Euan could do it very well. Then the drum left the ground and started flying through the air, while the duck and the tractor trundled along underneath.

But they had not gone very far when they saw a little man in a fur hat, who was rushing to and fro, to and fro, among a great many heaps of snow. When the man saw Euan he called out, 'Is that a drum you have there? Then you are just in time to take part in the contest.'

'What contest?' said Euan. His drum landed in a heap of snow and the tractor and the duck came up and sat beside him.

'We're trying to wake the army,' said the man in the fur hat. 'They've been asleep for a hundred and three years, but now the enemy are coming. The King is offering half his crown to any drummer who can wake the soldiers.'

'Where are they?' said Euan.

He could see two drummers waiting ready with their drums, but he couldn't see any army.

'Under the snow,' said the fur-hatted man. 'Right, drummer number one, PLAY!'

So the first drummer raised his drum-sticks and beat a tattoo on his drum: Rrrrrrrrrrrrrrr-tat-a-tat-tat-TAT.

Nothing happened, though he banged on his drum so hard that he burst it.

'Right,' said the fur-hatted man. 'Drummer number two, PLAY!'

The second drummer raised his drumsticks and beat a reveille on his drum: Brrrrrrrrrrr-rum-tum-tiddle-um-tum-TUM.

Nothing happened, except that he also broke his drum.

'Right,' said the fur-hatted man. 'Drummer number three, on your marks, get set, PLAY!'

Euan looked at his three presents, and thought, 'I can't play on the drum, because that's for riding. And I can't bang on the tractor, because it sings. So it must be the duck.'

The duck nodded, at that, and gave him a friendly wink of its twinkling black eye. So he picked up the drumsticks and thumped the duck on its back. And it went: Brrrrrrrrrrrrrr-brek-ek-ek-ex, co-ax,co-AX.

All the heaps of snow began to stir and shuffle. A hundred and three soldiers sat up and started shaking off the snow, yawning and rubbing their eyes. Then they stood up, took bows and arrows off their backs, bent the bows, and aimed the arrows.

'Where's the enemy?' said Euan.

'Thank you,' said Euan. 'But what can I do with half a crown? I can't wear it.'

'Half a crown is better than no head. Put it on the tractor's bonnet. It will come in handy some day, I daresay.'

So Euan did this, and then he and the tractor and the duck and the drum went on over the snowy hill. This time Euan rode on the duck. It was very comfortable, like riding on a haycart.

But they had not gone very far when they saw a lot of Romans, pulling on ropes.

'Is that a tractor that you have there?' called the chief Roman. 'Then you are just in time to help us, if you will be so kind. For we have got a dragon in our bath, and we can't pull it out.'

As well as Romans pulling on the ropes, there were camels and elephants and oxen, horses and mules and a bear and a gorilla and two ostriches, who were more trouble then help, because they kept burying their heads in the snow.

But nothing would shift the dragon. He lay on his back, looking very contented, with his eyes shut, and his feet and his tail sticking out. And the ropes kept breaking and the elephants kept slipping about in the snow. And the hot soapy water was slopping *everywhere*.

'My goodness,' said Euan. 'Perhaps it will have to be the tractor this time.' So he wound up the tractor with its starting-handle, and the tractor rolled up beside the dragon in the Roman bath, and began to sing, very loud and clear, in the dragon's ear.

> Ting-a-ling ting, ting, hey-ding-a-ding-a-ding
> Now's the time for dragons to take to the wing
> Breakfast is a-waiting, bacon is a-sputtering

Eggs are all a-boiling, crumpets are a-
buttering
Tea's in the teapot, cream that the
farmer made
Now's the time for dragons to take a
little marmalade.'

At that the dragon opened his eyes, pulled
out the plug with his claw, left the bath,
lightning-quick, with a tremendously loud
soapy swoosh, tossing great slops of water

everywhere, and flew away fast, dripping on
everybody as he passed over.

'Well,' said the chief Roman, 'he could
have done that more tidily. But still, thank
you, Euan. As a reward you can have half a
Roman holiday.'

'What can I do with a half holiday?' said
Euan.

'Put it under the duck's wing. I daresay
it'll come in handy some day.'

So Euan put it under the duck's wing
and then he and the tractor and the drum
and the duck went on their way.

The next thing they saw was Euan's Aunt
Bertha, but to start with Euan didn't know
it was his Aunt Bertha, for she was all
wound up into a huge tangle of knitting

wool as big as a haystack.

The only thing she could say, underneath all the wool, was 'Phoomph! Phoomph!'

'Goodness me,' said Euan. 'I think there is somebody inside all that wool.'

So he tied one end of the wool, which stuck out, to the drum, and then the drum began to spin round and round, round and round and round, round and round, and round and round, a hundred and three times, until it had spun all the wool into a big tidy ball, and there, at the other end, was Aunt Bertha, quite red in the face.

'Poof! It was hot in there,' she said. 'I thought I'd never get out. First the Abominable Snowmen marched past and unwound all my wool, and then the dragon flew over and tangled it all round me. I certainly am glad you came along, Euan.'

'Why, it's my Auntie Birthday,' said Euan, and he gave her a hug.

'And are you pleased with your tractor and your drum and your duck?'

'Yes, thank you,' said Euan, 'but I think there was a bit of a muddle. I wanted a duck that would go in my bath. And I wanted a drum that I could play on. And I wanted a tractor that I could ride on.'

At that Aunt Bertha began to laugh like mad.

'Oh what a silly woman I am,' she said. 'I'm always making mistakes like that. But never mind, we can easily put it right.'

So she got out her big brown mixing-bowl with the white inside, and she put Euan into it with the tractor and the duck and the drum, and she took her wishing-spoon with the little shield-shape on the back, and she began to stir.

She stirred and she mixed and she stirred, a hundred and three times, until Euan felt quite dizzy. He seemed to be falling through a white hole, and he shut his eyes tight, tight, tight, and when he opened them again it was morning and he was back in his bed.

Quick as quick he put his hand under his pillow. But all he found there was a crumble of sugar. So then he sat up and looked round the room.

At the end of his bed was a little tractor just his size that he could really ride on.

And on the table was a big drum that he could really play on, with two drumsticks. And perched on his windowsill was a beautiful white duck which, the minute he saw it, gave a loud quack! and flew across the room to sit on his quilt, smiling at him with its big yellow beak and its bright black eyes.

On the tractor's bonnet was a half crown, painted in gold.

As for the half Roman holiday, it was nowhere to be seen. But when Euan got to school that morning all his friends stood up and sang, 'Happy birthday, Euan.' And the teacher said, 'As it's Euan's birthday you can all have a half holiday and go home this afternoon.'

So all his friends went back with Euan and every single one had a ride on the tractor. And they played on his drum. And that night at bedtime the white duck came and swam in Euan's bath; and it perched on his windowsill all night long.

The Queen of the Moon

ONCE THERE WAS a girl called Tansy
whose father was a digger. Whenever people
wanted a road dug up, to lay pipes, or a
space cleared, to build a house, Tansy's
father, and other men as well, would do the
digging. Tansy hadn't any mother, so while
the men dug she found things to do on the
edge of the earthy, dusty place where they
were at work.

She built castles out of the stones they
dug up, or made patterns out of the bits of
glass and china. Sometimes she found old
arrowheads, or old broken clay pipes, or old
bones. Once or twice she found an old coin,
but her father always took those, saying he
would show them to a museum, and perhaps get money for them. Tansy never
heard if he did.

Tansy and her father never had much
money, because diggers don't get paid
much. They lived in a box on wheels that
was meant for moving horses. Tansy's
father had found it at a cross-roads, and,
as it was not too heavy to pull, he dragged
it away. It made a useful home; there was
room in it for two bunks, though not much
else.

When the weather was wet, Tansy and her
father had breakfast, mostly bread-and-
jam, lying in their bunks. When it was fine
they ate outside. And they pulled the
horse-box to wherever Tansy's father
happened to be doing his digging.

Just now he was digging in London, on a
huge wide space that would one day be
covered with a grand new vegetable market.
It was so big that there would be work for
months ahead, so he was pleased about the
job. Tansy was not so happy. She did not
care for this great open windy, dusty place
in the middle of the city.

'Shame about it, really,' her father said
once. 'Used to be all streets, here, long ago,
people's houses, lots of them. Your great-
great-grandma lived round here, years
back.'

'Did she?' said Tansy. 'What was her
name?'

'Dido, like your ma. But she married
some rich bloke and moved away.'

After that, Tansy hunted in the dust even
more carefully, in hopes she might find
something that had once belonged to her
great-great-grandma. And she did find a
little lead spoon that, if you looked very
hard and believed very hard, had something

scratched on it that might be the letters
D-I-D-O.

'What does Dido mean?' she asked her
father.

'Dunno,' he said, filling his pipe with
tobacco. 'Maybe it means died, like your
ma.'

But one of Tansy's father's mates, a boy
called Morgan who was digging to earn
money for college, said that Dido was a
queen's name.

Maybe the rich bloke that great-great-
grandma married was a king, Tansy
thought.

'What does Tansy mean?' she asked
Morgan.

A lady they had lodged with once, before
they got the horse-box, had said that Tansy
was a very odd name, and not at all
common.

'It's a flower, a kind of flower that grows
on waste places. It looks something like a
daisy.'

'What does a daisy look like?'

'Haven't you ever seen a *daisy*?'

'Dunno,' said Tansy. 'There aren't any
round here, are there?'

'No,' said Morgan, looking round the huge
dusty place where they stood. 'That's true.

Well, if your dad doesn't mind, I'll take you to see some on Sunday.'

Tansy's dad didn't mind at all. He liked to spend his Sundays sleeping. So on Sunday Tansy and Morgan caught a bus into the country, where Tansy had never been, for digging jobs are mostly in towns, and Tansy's dad always chose the town ones if he had a choice.

They got out of the bus and walked along a road, past a little church, and across a farmyard where hens were pecking about and doves sat on a wall, making a contented peaceful noise as if they were clearing their throats. Green feathery plants grew at the side of the yard. They had white-and-yellow flowers which gave off a strong musky sweetish smell in the warm sun.

'That's tansy,' said Morgan, 'that white-and-yellow stuff. And now – look – here's daisies.'

They had come to the edge of a field, where grass grew as high as Tansy's chest. Among the grass, and so thick that the field was white with them, were single flowers the size of eyes, or egg-yolks – hundreds and thousands and millions and billions and trillions of them. They had a calm smell

– not so sweet as the tansy, but comfortable, like toast. Up above the sun shone, and somewhere a bird hung in the sky and sang the same song over and over.

'Are these daisies?' Tansy looked at the flowers, which were almost up to her chin.

'Those are moon daisies.'

'I suppose they grow like that on the moon too.'

'Maybe.'

Tansy and Morgan ate the sausage rolls he had brought, and then he lay down in a clump of grass at the edge of the field and went to sleep. Tansy walked along the side of the field till she came to a little stream. She built a dam out of sticks and mud. Then she built an island out of stones, and put smaller stones and earth on top. Over the earth she laid green moss, and then she picked moon daisies and stuck them into the moss. They looked as if they were growing. She had to wade up to her knees, and her jeans got rather wet. She took off her vest to carry loads of stones and earth in it. The stones made more holes in the vest, but there had been holes in it anyway.

Then Morgan woke up and told her to put her vest back on, and they caught the bus back to London.

That night Tansy slept badly and she had a queer dream.

She dreamed that she was on the moon, which was as big and round as a circus ring, and flat and shining, and covered all over with white flowers.

In the middle, picking flowers, was a girl about Tansy's size.

'Hullo,' said this girl. 'I'm Dido. What's your name?'

'Tansy,' said Tansy.

'Oh, then you must be my great-great-grand-daughter.'

'I've got your spoon,' said Tansy, and took it out of her jeans pocket.

'So you have,' said Dido,

looking at it carefully. 'I used to eat my
porridge with that, when I lived in Nine
Elms. Now I'm Queen of the Moon.'

'Do you like that?'

'It's not bad. I can pick all the flowers I
want, and eat moon-candy and ice-cream
moondaes, and listen to the moon birds,
and ride moon-horses.'

'It's nice here,' said Tansy.

'Well you can come whenever you like, so
long as you have my spoon.'

'Thank you, great-great-grandma,' said
Tansy, putting the spoon back in her
pocket.

'That's all right,' Dido said. 'You can call
me Dido, if you like.'

Next day when Tansy woke she
remembered this dream. After that, she
always made sure that she had the little
lead spoon safe in her pocket.

That day, and for some days after, she felt
stiff and tired, and achey in her arms and
legs, so she didn't go out to the dusty site
where the men were digging, but lay in her
bunk and thought about the moon all
covered in white daisies.

Every night that week she dreamed about
the moon. Dido was there, and they picked
the white flowers, and rode the white

73

Tansy got back into bed, holding her little spoon tight, and when the nurse had gone she lay looking at the great silvery plateful of moon that hung in the sky just outside her window.

'Even if that isn't my moon,' she thought as her eyes closed, 'it's a nice colour. And I expect that Mr Smith's right. I'm sure to find my own moon somewhere, with Dido on it.'